THE BLACK BE

Beware of the
Haunted Eye

The dojo at Karate Kids World

THE BLACK BELT CLUB

Beware of the Haunted Eye

DAWN BARNES

illustrated by

BERNARD CHANG

THE BLUE SKY PRESS
An Imprint of Scholastic Inc. • New York

THE BLUE SKY PRESS

Text copyright © 2007 by Dawn Barnes
Illustrations copyright © 2007 by Dawn Barnes
All rights reserved.

Special thanks to Robert Martin Staenberg.

SCHOLASTIC, THE BLUE SKY PRESS, and associated logos
are trademarks and/or registered trademarks of Scholastic Inc.

Library of Congress catalog card number available.

ISBN-10: 0-439-85657-4 / ISBN-13: 978-0-439-85657-7

10 9 8 7 6 5 4 3   08 09 10 11
Printed in the United States of America 40

First printing, April 2007

In aligning with the theme of this book,

I honor the matriarchal influences in my life—

Mommanina, Aunt Nancy, Bernice, Alesia, and Bonnie.

Thank you for your grace and wisdom.

—D.B.

For Bob Layton, Steve Massarsky, Jon Hartz,

Martin Stever, and Fred Pierce.

Special thanks to Bonnie, Dawn, Kathleen,

Tom, and Ha.

—B.C.

CHAPTER 1

I'M SCARED. Sensei said she was going to test us today on the ten-step kicking set. I know I'm going to mess up—I did really badly on the last test.

I waited and waited for Uncle Al to pick me up after school, but he never showed. This isn't the first time. I really miss my dad. He travels a lot on business to China. He keeps saying he's going to take me with him someday. That would be so cool, but he hasn't come home from China in a long time. Living with Uncle Al is awful. He never wants to go anywhere. He just likes to watch TV.

Since Uncle Al didn't come, I took the bus to

Karate Kids World. I didn't want to be late for our training. I made it to the dojo just in time.

Right now, there are only four of us in the Black Belt Club. Antonio, Maia, and Jamie were already on the mat, talking with Sensei. I quickly put on my karate *gi* and joined them.

HELLO, SENSEI.

GOOD AFTERNOON, MAX. NOW THAT YOU'RE HERE, LET'S LINE UP AND DO SOME STRETCHES SO WE CAN PRACTICE THE KICKING SET.

MAX, CAN YOU REMEMBER ALL *TEN* MOVES?

"I think so," I answered. I did so badly last time that I've been practicing really hard. "It's front kick, slide-up side kick, pivoting side kick, and then . . ."

"And then what?" asked Antonio.

"Um, I forget. That's weird."

"This is what I'm talking about. None of us can remember past the first three moves."

"Kiotsuki, rei." Sensei gave the command to bow.

I sat next to Jamie and reached for my toes. "What comes after the first three moves?" I asked her.

I CAN'T REMEMBER. EVEN AT HOME THIS MORNING, I COULDN'T REMEMBER MORE THAN THREE THINGS. I GOT UP, BRUSHED MY TEETH, MADE MY BED, AND THEN I FORGOT WHAT I USUALLY DO NEXT.

WHEN I WAS IN SCHOOL TODAY, I COULDN'T **CONCENTRATE** ON ANYTHING THE TEACHER SAID.

"So what else is new?" asked Maia.

She's got a real attitude. But Antonio was used to it. He ignored her.

"Jump up, everyone. Let's move our bodies and see if that helps our minds," said Sensei. "I will now demonstrate the ten-step kicking set."

Sensei stepped from one kick to the next with speed and power, calling out each technique before she did it. We followed right behind her, copying her every move.

FRONT KICK

SLIDE-UP SIDE KICK

PIVOTING SIDE KICK

STEPPING SIDE KICK

SPINNING BACK KICK

HOPPING BACK KICK

HOOK KICK

CRESCENT KICK

STOMP KICK

DROPPING MULE KICK

KIAI!!!

"Hey, we did it!" said Antonio.

"Very good," said Sensei. "All day today my students seemed to be forgetting their moves—and I've had a hard time, too. So we need to concentrate as much as we can. Now, let me see you one at a time."

I hate this part. Everyone always does it perfectly, and I always mess up.

"Max, you're first," she said.

Just then, we heard the faint sound of chimes coming from the corner cabinet.

Phew! Saved by the bell. But, then again, maybe not. I know what that bell means. We're being called to another mission. And missions worry me—a lot!

CIRCLE TIME.

My stomach was churning. *The kicking set is nothing compared to these missions.*

She unlocked the cabinet and carefully brought the Box of the Four Doors to the center of the room. She lifted the acorn lid, and inside the five secret compartments were our crystals. Each of us has our own Animal Power, and our crystals help us to connect to them.

"Everyone, take your crystal out of the box, and hold it up to the light," said Sensei.

Sensei chose the center crystal and held it high. It was clear, but inside it reflected a rainbow of colors. Antonio, Maia, Jamie, and I took our crystals and held them up to the light. As our crystals touched, a spark of energy lit the room. The Box of the Four Doors began to spin. We watched it spin faster and faster, and then it suddenly stopped.

Pop! The north-facing door fell open, and a small hologram appeared. It was a crystal ball with a woman standing in the center of it. Her skin and hair were white, and she wore a long white gown. A circle of flowers lay like a crown on her head.

ALLARIA!

I looked at Sensei, and for the first time ever, I saw fear in her eyes.

"How could this be?" she asked.

"We are not sure, but your four champions are needed," Allaria continued. "The evil force has been released into our forest. The creatures are hypnotized and have lost their focus. They have forgotten what they are supposed to do, and why. It will soon be too late for all of us. Your Black Belt Club must come now to the Isle of Oculus."

Allaria put her head down. The crystal ball became cloudy, and she faded away.

Sensei stood up, and I was the only one left sitting. I held my crystal tight. *Why do I always get so nervous before these missions? They're really scary, that's why!*

"Sensei, what exactly is *it*?" I asked.

"The Haunted Eye," she said softly.

The room fell silent.

THE HAUNTED EYE WAS CAPTURED AND HIDDEN LONG AGO, OUT OF SIGHT FROM ALL LIGHT SO IT COULD NOT LOOK UPON THE LAND OR THE CREATURES OF THE FOREST.

WHAT HAPPENS IF IT DOES?

THE HAUNTED EYE IS AN EVIL ENERGY FORCE. *OCULUS* IS A PLACE WHERE NATURE IS SACRED. THE PATTERN OF THE SEASONS MAY CHANGE, AND ALL LIFE COULD DIE. WE MUST STOP THE HAUNTED EYE. THERE IS NO TIME TO LOSE. MAX, IT IS YOUR DECISION IF YOU STAY OR GO.

IT'S NO BIG DEAL IF YOU WANT TO STAY BEHIND, MAX. MAYBE YOU SHOULD JUST GO HOME TODAY.

She gave me that look that she always gives me. The one that says, "I know you're a chicken, Max. Just admit it."

"I'm good," I said. I squeezed the crystal in my hands. *But I'm not going without my Animal Power.*

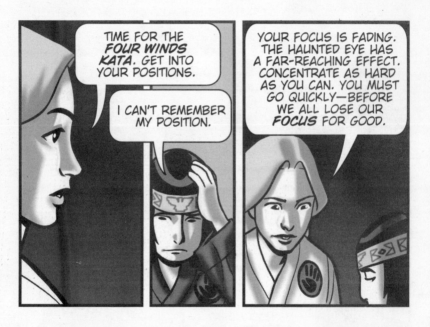

I usually can't remember what to do anyway, so what's the difference? I thought. *Maybe I should just go home.*

"Max," said Sensei, bringing me out of my daze. "Are you with us?"

If your idea of fun is traps, danger, and nearly dying, I thought. But I couldn't help myself. "Sure, Antonio," I said. "I'm in."

Sensei led us to our four directions so we could begin our special kata. I was in the North, Antonio was in the South, Maia was in the East, and Jamie was in the West.

I KNOW YOU ARE HAVING TROUBLE FOCUSING, SO CALL UPON YOUR ANIMAL POWERS TO GUIDE YOU THROUGH THE FOUR WINDS KATA. TRY YOUR BEST!

NOW HOLD YOUR CRYSTALS HIGH TO THE SKY, AND CLOSE YOUR EYES. PICTURE YOUR ANIMAL MOVING TOWARD YOU IN YOUR MIND. ONCE IT IS BESIDE YOU, PUT YOUR HAND UPON IT. FEEL YOUR ANIMAL'S POWER AS IT GUIDES YOU THROUGH THE KATA.

I focused hard to call my animal to me.

I opened one eye and peeked at the others. We held our crystals while we moved through the kata. Light streamed in the windows and lit up the animals inside our stones. I closed my eyes and imagined my Bear standing next to me. As soon as I did, I felt my muscles strengthen. *My Bear was with me!*

I opened my eyes, and everyone looked stronger. We circled one another in our dance-like kata. Maia had the perfect balance of a crane as she did five spinning kicks in a row without falling. Jamie looked like an eagle—light on her feet, as if she were flying and striking at the same time. Antonio just looked mean. *Whoa. I wouldn't want to get in his way!* He did stomping kicks that were so hard I felt the floor shake under my feet! *I'm never that good. But I do feel extra strong right now.*

Out of the corner of my eye, I saw Sensei watching. We were going fast, and our kata was taking us to a different time, apart from her. But I read her lips and saw her say, "May the four winds guide you and keep you safe!"

And, in a flash of wind and light, we were gone.

CHAPTER 2

"AH!"

We jumped and dodged bodies rolling at us from every direction.

"What's going on?" I yelled.

"Jump!" screamed Maia.

She and Antonio leaped away just in time. Martial artists tumbled back and forth across the mat like human bowling balls. We had landed in the middle of a giant dojo where masked attackers dressed in green were trying to knock us down. They flipped and rolled so fast we barely had time to get out of the way.

"Side step, quick!" yelled Jamie. But it was too late. I was knocked down by a whirling body. I fell hard on my back, but I broke the fall. I threw my arms out to the side and slapped the mat the exact second I hit the ground.

Suddenly, we were surrounded by six warriors. They wore strange green karate uniforms and plant-like masks.

"Haaa!" The signal was given. The group rolled straight toward the center of the circle. We stood upright like bowling pins, ready to be knocked down!

"Flying side kicks over their backs!" yelled Maia. "Go!"

We leaped into the air just as they rolled beneath us. They jumped up, ready to strike again. Then they stopped. From the far end of the mat, they glared at us from behind their masks.

DID THE FOUR WINDS KATA BRING US TO THE RIGHT PLACE?

THIS IS A STRANGE WAY TO SAY HELLO.

I BET THE *HAUNTED EYE* IS CONTROLLING THEM.

The warriors suddenly **stood** upright and at attention. Then they bowed.

"Yeah, that's right," said Antonio. "It's about time you showed a little respect."

"Respect goes both ways," said a voice behind us. A man and a woman stood near the doorway. They bowed slightly to the warriors, and then the warriors quickly left the room.

ALLARIA!

WELCOME TO THE *ISLE OF OCULUS.*

I HOPE OUR WARRIORS DIDN'T FRIGHTEN YOU. THEY WERE PRACTICING, AND YOU LANDED RIGHT IN THE MIDDLE OF THEIR DRILLS.

LET ME INTRODUCE YOU TO *KAELIN*, CHIEF INSTRUCTOR IN THE *HOUSE OF THE GREEN WARRIORS.*

Kaelin wore a helmet that hid his eyes. It gave him a menacing appearance. He also wore a battle vest made of studded leather, and a thick belt hung from his hips. Attached to the belt was a scabbard holding a long sword. On his shoulders he wore a gold cape that made him look like a king, or an officer of high military rank.

"Pleased to make your acquaintance," Kaelin said with a bow.

As he lifted his head, chills ran up and down my body. Suddenly, I felt tense. I wanted to run away from him. Maia and Jamie giggled.

She's acting tough, but she's definitely blushing.

"I beg your pardon. Then you have come to the right place. We must train together and compare our fighting styles."

"Hopefully there will be no fighting," said Allaria.

"Of course, Priestess," said Kaelin. "That is always our hope."

I could tell he was lying. I could tell he really did want to fight.

WELL, WE ARE ALL ON THE SAME SIDE, ARE WE NOT?

"What is a priestess?" asked Jamie.

"A teacher and a guide," Allaria answered.

"That's what Sensei calls herself," said Maia. "Is she a priestess, too?"

"She and I learned many arts together, including martial arts and the Art of Sight and Focus."

"Is that like seeing the future?" I asked.

"Sometimes."

"Can you teach us that?" asked Antonio.

IT'S NOT ALWAYS A GOOD THING TO KNOW WHAT MIGHT HAPPEN AHEAD OF TIME.

YOUR SENSEI AND I HAVE LEARNED THAT THE FUTURE CAN BE CHANGED. WHAT YOU DO NOW IS THE MOST IMPORTANT THING. COME. LET ME SHOW YOU SOMETHING.

CHAPTER 3

WE STEPPED outside into a large courtyard surrounded by two stone buildings. Climbing up the stones were thick vines. On top of the main building was a giant glass dome. Light rays beamed back and forth across it.

"This is the House of Sight," Allaria told us.

"Sweet!" said Antonio. "It's like one of those laser light shows at the planetarium."

We followed Allaria through a doorway and into the House of Sight. We entered a large hall with a row of columns leading into the dome. People came in and out from side doors. They carried books, plants, and trays of stones. Each of them wore a robe, and each robe had an eye embroidered across the chest.

"Eyes everywhere," I said.

"It's kind of creepy," Jamie said, looking at the engravings on the walls.

"It's as if the eyes are watching us," I said.

Everyone we passed bowed as Priestess Allaria walked by.

At the far end of the hall, we climbed a spiral staircase that was three stories high, and we entered the Dome of Sight. At the very top was an opening to the sky. It, also, was shaped like an eye.

THIS IS DEFINITELY A ROOM WITH A VIEW.

Through glass windows, we could see in every direction. Gardens and spiral paths twisted back and forth in an endless pattern. Beyond them, the forest went on forever.

"Look at all the trails and hedges," said Jamie. "It's a giant maze. I think I'd get lost in there."

"It's a labyrinth," said Maia. "And yes, it's probably very complicated to figure out."

"What's a labyrinth?" asked Antonio.

"A complex pattern, like a puzzle, that will take teamwork to solve," Allaria told us all. "In our world, all heroes must find their way through the maze to prove their powers of focus."

She was standing in the center of the room. Beside her, on an elaborate stand, was a large crystal ball.

I COME TO THE **DOME OF SIGHT** TO FOCUS UPON THE PAST, THE PRESENT, AND THE FUTURE. PEOPLE FROM MANY WORLDS COME TO ME FOR ADVICE. BUT UNFORTUNATELY, I AM NOT MUCH USE TO THEM RIGHT NOW.

"What do you mean?" I asked.

She closed her eyes and put both hands on the crystal ball. Bright images began to appear and disappear inside of it. But just as the pictures began to sharpen, the ball suddenly filled with clouds. The images were gone. Allaria jerked her hands away from the crystal ball as if it had given her an electrical shock. She gasped and sat down.

WHY IS IT CALLED THE HAUNTED EYE? IS IT *HAUNTED*?

IN OUR WORLD, THE EYES CONNECT TO OUR SPIRIT POWER, THE STRENGTH WE HAVE INSIDE US. THE HAUNTED EYE TAKES OVER OUR FOCUS, AND IT CAPTURES SPIRIT POWER. ANYONE LOOKING INTO THE EYE WILL FORGET HIS OWN POWER.

CAN ANYONE GET HIS SPIRIT POWER BACK?

ONLY IF THE HAUNTED EYE IS CAPTURED BEFORE THE FIRST RAYS OF SUNLIGHT SHINE ON THE FIRST DAY OF SPRING— THE SPRING EQUINOX.

BUT ON THAT DAY, THE KING OF THE FOREST, THE GREEN MAN, MUST BE THE FIRST TO SEE DAYLIGHT IN ORDER FOR SPRINGTIME TO BEGIN.

AND WHAT HAPPENS IF THE HAUNTED EYE SEES THE LIGHT FIRST?

THEN ITS EVIL WILL RULE OVER THE LAND. OURS IS A WORLD OF NATURE AND FOCUS. ALL MEMORY WILL BE LOST. THE SEASONS WILL NOT CHANGE.

NO MORE SEASONS?

NO SUMMER?

THE *CYCLES OF LIFE* WILL BE OUT OF BALANCE, AND MANY CREATURES WILL DIE.

We looked at one another. No one said a word.

"I am afraid that many creatures in the forest have already been hypnotized," said Allaria.

"How do you know?" I asked.

"In our forest, there is a ruler: the Green Man. But lately, the Green Man has not been himself. He runs wild and threatens to hurt the creatures. We are worried that he is under the spell of the Haunted Eye," said Allaria.

WHAT IS THE GREEN MAN SUPPOSED TO DO?

WHAT IS THE STONE CIRCLE?

HE PROTECTS THE PLANTS, ANIMALS, AND OTHER FOREST BEINGS. HE IS THE KING OF THE NATURAL WORLD. EVERY THREE MONTHS WHEN IT IS TIME FOR THE SEASONS TO CHANGE, HE AND I MEET AT THE STONE CIRCLE TO PREDICT WHAT THE NEW SEASON MIGHT BRING.

IT IS A SPECIAL PLACE HIGH ON A HILL, MARKED BY A CIRCLE OF STONES. IT IS THE FIRST PLACE THE SUN SHINES WHEN IT RISES IN OUR WORLD.

WHAT EXACTLY DO YOU DO THERE?

WE TRY TO PREDICT THE NEW SEASON—THE RAIN, HEAT, AND COLD, AND THE EFFECT OF THE MOON AND STARS. THIS HELPS US TO KNOW HOW MANY NEW BIRDS WILL BE BORN, WHAT NEW TREES WILL GROW, AND WHAT THE ANIMALS AND OTHER CREATURES OF THE FOREST WILL NEED TO DO TO MAKE THE SEASON SAFE AND HARMONIOUS.

THE ANIMALS DO THINGS TO MAKE YOUR WORLD HARMONIOUS?

YES. IN OUR WORLD, ALL CREATURES WORK TOGETHER FOR THE GOOD OF THE WHOLE.

I heard footsteps on the stairs. I turned to see Kaelin enter the room. "Greetings, Priestess. I suggest our visitors have some training before they begin their journey."

"I'm afraid these students don't have any time for training today, Kaelin," said Allaria. "They must begin their journey while it is still daylight."

He walked over to Allaria and put his hand on her shoulder. "Priestess, I see that the clouded crystal has made you tired. Perhaps you should rest."

YES, I SHALL. BUT FIRST I MUST GIVE THEM THEIR THREE *GIFTS*.

I CAN TAKE CARE OF THAT. WHY DON'T YOU REST? I CAN FINISH HERE.

I could tell this was a bad idea.

"Priestess Allaria," I said. "It would really mean a lot to me to get the gifts from you." I gave her my biggest and brightest smile.

Under his helmet, I could hear Kaelin growl.

"Please," I said. "It would be more special."

She smiled back at me. "With such pleasant manners, how can I refuse?"

Kaelin turned, then stomped away. "I will see you soon, my friends," he barked over his shoulder.

Allaria ran her hands over her crystal ball. An eye appeared inside it. "This is your first gift. If you each touch my crystal ball with your own crystals, yours will have the gift of sight. They will light up to direct you to the Ley Lines that lead to the Stone Circle. Only in Oculus will you have this gift."

THANK YOU!

WHAT ARE *LEY LINES*?

THEY ARE LINES OF ENERGY UNDER THE GROUND. IF YOU FOLLOW THEM, YOU WILL REACH THE STONE CIRCLE.

I held my crystal up to the dome, and suddenly it lit up. I could see my Bear—my Animal Power —etched inside.

"Whoa!" said Antonio. He looked at his crystal and closed his hands around it. "My Bull! Wait a minute. What makes it light up, without a ray of sun?"

"The Ley Lines have enormous energy in nature —and they connect you to your animal powers, to help you," said Allaria.

I stared into my crystal, and my Bear looked back at me. I instantly felt calm, and my usual nervousness was gone. *This is definitely a good thing.*

"Remember, this is a tool to use if you get lost," she said. "It will always guide you to the Ley Lines."

Lost? My stomach knotted. *Here we go again. Another mission of doom!* I held my crystal tight.

Allaria gave each of us a leather pouch. I tied mine to my belt and put my crystal inside.

NOW, FOR YOUR SECOND GIFT.

She opened a nearby closet. Inside were four brown capes. Each had a swirling design around the edges of the hood.

"The design on this cape is called the triple-knot. It has the power to stop the Haunted Eye from looking into your eyes. This is very important for your safety. It can save you from becoming hypnotized."

HOW?

THE KNOT HAS NO BEGINNING AND NO END. IT IS ONE CONSTANT *SWIRL*. WHEN THE EYE TRIES TO FOLLOW THE PATTERN, IT NEVER STOPS MOVING. THAT WAY, IT WILL NOT BE ABLE TO *FOCUS* ON YOU.

AND THEN, HOPEFULLY, WE CAN KEEP OUR *SPIRIT POWER!*

We each took a cape and put it on. Then we looked out over the labyrinth forest.

"What's the third gift, Allaria?" asked Maia.

"It's the most difficult to remember. But it will remind you of how you need to think in order to capture the Haunted Eye."

"What is it?" asked Jamie.

"It's . . . it's . . . it's . . . " Allaria's voice grew faint, and she touched her head. "I'm losing my focus again. And I'm so tired. . . . I can't seem to remember it right now."

"Then how do we get it?" asked Maia.

"There is another way. You will pass through the maze and then through the forest. When you come to a village, a man can help you. . . . Lyric . . . will remember. He can . . . teach the third gift to you. . . . "

Allaria swayed a little. Maia grabbed her arm to steady her.

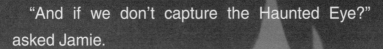

"And if we don't capture the Haunted Eye?" asked Jamie.

"Total darkness," I answered.

"Yes," said Allaria, faintly. "Total darkness for a thousand years."

CHAPTER 4

WE STOOD at the entrance to the labyrinth, a maze made of thick hedges. This would lead us to the forest. Three paths opened before us, and each would send us in a different direction.

"It's going to be impossible for us to find our way through!" I said.

"Thinking positive as usual, Max?" said Maia.

"You should talk!" Antonio said.

"Come on, you guys—focus!" said Jamie.

"Fine. Allaria gave us two tools," said Maia.

"A special power to light our crystals, and capes," said Jamie.

SHE TOLD US HOW TO USE THE CAPE.

BUT I'M NOT SURE HOW TO USE THE LIGHT INSIDE MY CRYSTAL.

ALLARIA SAID THE LIGHT WILL GUIDE US.

YEAH, BUT HOW?

I took my crystal out of my pouch and held it up to the middle pathway.

"Why isn't it glowing?" I asked. "It lit up in the Dome of Sight."

The others held out their crystals. Jamie walked over to the left path, and Maia went to the right path. Jamie's crystal stayed dark, but Maia's lit up.

LOOK AT MY CRYSTAL!

IT'S GIVING US DIRECTIONS!

THIS MUST BE A *LEY LINE* TO THE STONE CIRCLE.

We entered the maze through the right path. Tall hedges lined the trail on both sides of us. We couldn't see anything except for the path. There was no turning back now.

Somewhere in this forest lurks the Haunted Eye. How on earth are we supposed to capture an eyeball? Won't it be squishy and gross? And why is there always some really scary bad guy on these missions? Why can't we just go do something normal? I wondered.

SO WE FOLLOW THIS TRAIL AND HOPE WE GET LUCKY?

ALLARIA SAID WE HAVE THE TOOLS WE NEED FOR OUR JOURNEY. SOMETIMES YOU HAVE TO *TRUST*.

Trust. Hmm. I don't know about that.

Boom! The sound of thunder erupted.

"Where did that come from?" asked Jamie.

We stood in silence and felt the ground rumble under our feet.

"It's coming from the right," said Antonio.

"No, it's coming from the left," said Maia.

I turned and looked behind us. "Run!"

Hot on our trail was a stampede of deer. They had huge, pointed antlers. Leading the team was a very strange creature. He looked like a human tree—he was tall, thin, and made of vines from head to toe. He rode the largest deer—the king stag.

WHO DARES TO ENTER MY LABYRINTH?

He kicked the stag harder. "Faster! Faster!"

"That must be the Green Man!" I yelled. "But he's trying to catch us!" *Somehow I'm always the last in line and the first in danger!*

We sprinted as fast as we could. I kept watch for an escape route, but the hedge was solid. The hoofbeats grew louder. I heard the Green Man laugh, but it wasn't friendly.

WHY ARE WE RUNNING AWAY?

WE'RE SUPPOSED TO CHECK HIM OUT AND SEE IF HE'S BEEN *HYPNOTIZED*.

WE NEED A PLAN SO WE DON'T GET TRAMPLED!

TAG TEAM!

TWO OF US ON EACH SIDE OF THE TRAIL!

GOT IT! WHEN HE RIDES PAST, YOU AND MAIA DO A FLYING SIDE KICK AND KNOCK HIM OFF THE STAG. THEN MAX AND I WILL GRAB HIM ON THE OTHER SIDE!

BUT WE'RE NOT SUPPOSED TO HURT HIM! WHAT ARE YOU DOING?

Just then, the Green Man roared in a voice that filled the forest. "Get them!" he cried.

"He's hypnotized for sure!" Antonio yelled. "Let's get him first!"

"Speak for yourself, Antonio. I think running is the best idea!" I yelled.

"OK, team!" shouted Maia. "Split apart, and get ready!"

We ran to opposite sides of the path and stopped. I tried to catch my breath.

WHAT ABOUT THE HAUNTED EYE?

IF YOU SEE IT, MAKE SURE YOU DON'T LOOK AT IT. HEY, EVERYONE! PUT YOUR HOODS UP, JUST IN CASE.

We stood ready and faced the oncoming stags. The Green Man roared, "You won't escape me now! Your spirit power will be mine!"

As he rode closer, I saw the Haunted Eye! It was mounted on a crown on his head. The Eye was as big as a football! It had red, bulging veins, and it dripped blood down onto the Green Man's face.

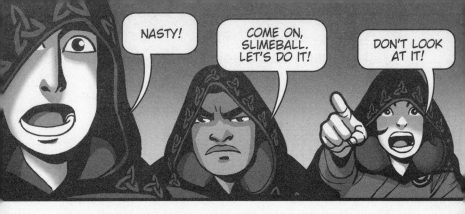

I pulled my hood above my eyes. I hoped the Haunted Eye would look at the triple-knot design instead of me. But Antonio forgot to cover his eyes. The Haunted Eye stared right at him. A screaming sound came out of the Eye. It could talk!

MAX! WHAT ARE WE ARE DOING AGAIN?

OH, NO! IT'S STEALING YOUR FOCUS! ANTONIO, LOOK AWAY! LOOK AT ME! CONCENTRATE! THE GIRLS ARE KICKING THE GREEN MAN OFF THE STAG, AND WE'RE SUPPOSED TO CATCH HIM, REMEMBER?

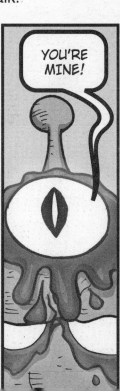

YOU'RE MINE!

Just in time, Antonio looked at me. He shook his head, trying to think. "OK. . . . I remember now."

"On the count of three," commanded Maia.

The stampede was going to reach us in six seconds. The ground shook from their stomping hooves.

"He's almost here. Ready? *Ichi, ni, san!*" Maia yelled in Japanese.

We timed it perfectly. Just as the Green Man rode between us, the girls flipped up into the air and side kicked him to the ground. We pressed the Green Man against the hedge to let the herd run past. But he didn't stay down for long. His limbs stretched out like a plant growing at superspeed. He whipped his vine-like arms up to the sky. Then he quickly wrapped them around Maia.

The Green Man's leg suddenly reached out and snapped at Antonio like a rattlesnake. His head jerked from side to side as the Eye tried to capture our focus.

"You are all cowards!" the Haunted Eye rasped. "You are afraid to look at me, you weak, snotty children! Get out of my labyrinth!" The Green Man's eyes rolled back in his head. All the time I'd thought it was the Green Man yelling, but it was really the Haunted Eye!

Jamie and I did our best board-breaking karate chops on the vines squeezing Maia and Antonio. But the vines were too thick.

"We know that the Green Man is good," Jamie said. "Surrender now, and you will stay in one piece!"

The Evil Eye hissed. Then the Green Man's body stretched upward until he was as tall as an oak tree! He let Maia and Antonio go, and branches began to sprout from his gigantic, tree-like body. He spun round and round like a tornado. His legs, like roots, whipped the dirt up into a cyclone, and it flew into our eyes.

I could just make out Maia's voice. "Lunge, now! Sweep him off his feet, and then grab the Eye! Go!"

I threw myself into a forward shoulder roll and tried to hit his root-like legs. I tumbled hard and hit something. I got him! I held on tight to what felt like a leg. The sound of screaming circled in the swirling wind tunnel around my head, but I couldn't understand the words. Then, suddenly, it all stopped. I coughed the dust out of my lungs and looked down at what I had tackled. It was Antonio!

"Get off me, Max!"

"Sorry, Antonio! I thought you were the . . . where is he?"

We looked around. The Green Man and the Haunted Eye were gone!

CHAPTER 5

WE TRAVELED deeper into the labyrinth. The Green Man and the Haunted Eye were nowhere in sight.

"The Green Man is probably headed for the Stone Circle," said Maia.

"The problem is that we don't know how to get through this maze," said Antonio.

"Hopefully our crystals will lead us," said Jamie.

There's that word again: "hopefully." I've hoped for a lot of things, and they usually don't happen. But I do know from our other missions that I need to try to think positively. All we can do is try our best.

I pulled out my crystal. It was still glowing. "I guess we keep going this way," I said.

"Let's jog. It's almost sundown," said Antonio.

As we ran through the crooked maze of hedges, we soon came to another fork in the path.

THE TRAIL SPLITS HERE. LET'S ALL HOLD UP OUR CRYSTALS.

The crystals lit up when pointed at the path to the left. We continued to run. The trail twisted and turned and forked several more times until we felt as if we were going in circles. As soon as we slowed down to catch our breath, the hedges on both sides began to close in around us. We jumped into ready stance.

Suddenly, the hedge in front of us exploded!

"The Green Man!" I yelled.

He stretched his tree-like body high to the sky, but not before he scooped us up in his vine-like arms and shoved us up in front of him. We were facing the Haunted Eye!

"Don't look at it!" yelled Maia.

The hood on my cape had fallen back, so I tried to keep my head down to avoid the Eye. The Green Man pulled us closer. *There's no escape,* I thought. *Time's up. I'm going to lose my spirit power!*

WELL, WELL. LOOKS LIKE MY FRIENDS WERE LOST IN THE FOREST, AND NOW THEY'RE FOUND.

We looked down and saw Kaelin!

"They were sent to capture me," hissed the Haunted Eye. "You were a fool to let them go."

"Allaria's power stopped me," said Kaelin. "What shall we do with them now?"

KAELIN! HELP US!

HELP YOU? **WHY** WOULD I DO THAT?

I KNEW IT!

I TOLD YOU I HAD A **BAD** FEELING ABOUT HIM.

YOU'RE SUPPOSED TO BE ON **OUR** SIDE!

THE HAUNTED EYE HAS TAKEN YOU OVER!

YOU'RE ALLARIA'S TRUSTED FRIEND. YOU CAN'T BE THAT **EVIL**.

THE **EYE** IS GOOD.

ALLARIA DOESN'T UNDERSTAND IT, BUT I DO. WHO DO YOU THINK OPENED THE WELL OF MYSTERY AND LET THE EYE OUT FROM ITS PRISON?

I heard music somewhere in the distance—or was it a humming sound? I strained to turn my head. Moving toward us at lightning speed was a strange red cloud.

Antonio struggled to get free. "What's that noise?"

Hundreds of red grasshoppers swarmed around our heads. I shut my eyes as tight as I could. But instead of chewing into us, they stabbed at the Haunted Eye instead.

"Allaria must be behind this," Kaelin shouted, and the Haunted Eye screeched. The Green Man dropped us as his twisting arms flew to his face for protection. That was when I noticed the familiar triple-knot pattern on the grasshoppers.

Ahh! We fell through the air. I grabbed onto loose vines as I fell, hoping to slow myself down.

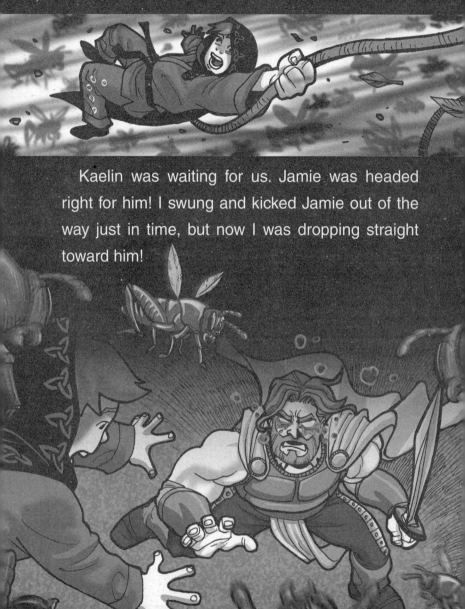

Kaelin was waiting for us. Jamie was headed right for him! I swung and kicked Jamie out of the way just in time, but now I was dropping straight toward him!

Antonio and Maia had landed safely and rushed at Kaelin. I grabbed another vine and swung away from him, just missing his blade.

Jamie ran to my side. "Good job, Max. Let's get him!" she said.

We surrounded Kaelin.

EVEN WITH FOUR AGAINST ONE, YOU DON'T HAVE A CHANCE. YOU'RE JUST *CHILDREN*.

WE'RE KIDS, BUT WE ARE ALSO THE *BLACK BELT CLUB*!

"Kiai!" we yelled, jumping into ready stance.

We circled Kaelin and tried to find an opening. He still had his sword drawn. He swung it back and forth so we couldn't get near him.

Meanwhile, the Green Man stumbled to the side, trying to protect his face and the Haunted Eye from the grasshoppers. I heard a loud horn blow in the distance. For the first time, Kaelin looked afraid. The horn sounded again.

"Let's go, Green Man. It's not time for this battle yet," Kaelin said. He waved his sword wildly in a circle to push us farther away from him. Then he leaped next to the Green Man. He lowered his helmet and quickly sheathed his sword.

I DOUBT WE WILL MEET AGAIN.

THOUGH YOU WERE SPARED MY SWORD, YOU WON'T SURVIVE THE MAZE—OR THE *FOREST*.

Then Kaelin and the Green Man ran through a small tunnel of thorny branches at the bottom of a hedge.

"Yeah, you better run!" yelled Antonio.

Now the horn was right behind us.

"No, *we* better run!" I yelled.

The hedge beside us rustled wildly, and the sound of the blasting horn was deafening.

The Green Man had knocked down one side of the hedges that led to a new trail.

"That way! Quick!" said Maia.

CHAPTER 6

WE RAN, and the sound of the horn seemed to get farther away. We looped back and forth along the winding path until the trail made one final triple loop. Then it opened up to a field covered with oak trees, small round houses, and grassy mounds. Each mound had a door on it.

"We made it through the labyrinth!" Maia cried. "And we escaped that horn!"

She and Antonio slapped a high five. Beyond the mounds, we could see the forest.

"Are those mounds houses?" I asked.

"Look at all the people—they're so little!" said Jamie.

The village people were very small—the tallest one was only the height of my shoulders. Each one was dressed in green and wore a different kind of hat.

Blam! Suddenly, the horn blasted right behind our heads.

AH!

We jumped. A gigantic ram's horn was being held up by a dozen of the villagers. The man blowing the horn seemed to be their leader.

"What is this, Santa's Village?" asked Maia.

The man blasted on the horn again.

"Stop that!" yelled Maia. "You're hurting our ears!"

WE WANTED TO SCARE AWAY THE HAUNTED EYE—THEN MAKE YOU FOCUS TO GET YOUR ATTENTION.

WELL, YOU'VE GOT IT.

HA! HA! HA! HA! HA! HA! HA!

WHO ARE YOU, AND WHAT DO YOU WANT?

I AM *LYRIC.*

LYRIC!

PRIESTESS ALLARIA TOLD US WE WOULD FIND YOU.

ALLARIA HAS SENT YOU ON A DIFFICULT JOURNEY. WE HAVE ALL BEEN *WEAKENED* BY THE HAUNTED EYE. THE LOUD SOUND OF THE HORN HELPS US, JUST AS IT HELPED LEAD YOU HERE TO SAFETY.

As we followed Lyric farther into the village, I noticed that all kinds of birds and small animals filled the surrounding oak trees. They sang together, making chattering sounds I had never heard before.

64

Everyone in the village was busy.

"What are they doing?" I asked.

"We are preparing for tomorrow—the spring equinox," answered Lyric.

People were cooking food, washing clothes, and making small fires next to their mound-houses to keep warm. It was almost dark, and some of the villagers climbed ladders to light lanterns that hung from the smaller oak trees. A full moon was rising in the east, and it cast shadows across the mounds. More strange animal sounds came from the forest beyond us.

"The animals are gathering for the sunrise ceremony," Lyric said. "Come in, but watch your head."

He led us to the door of a mound-house. We stepped inside.

"Is the third gift a song?" I asked. *I hope not. I'm a terrible singer.*

"No," said Lyric, and he bolted the door.

Antonio signaled me with his eyes. "I'm sorry, Lyric, but we need the third gift, and we need it now. Have you been hypnotized, too?"

I knew it was too good to be true. We jumped up into ready stance.

KIAI!

Lyric laughed at us. "Sit! I am Allaria's friend. I saw Kaelin attack you in the labyrinth. He was afraid we would tell you how to defeat the Haunted Eye. Now he is on the run."

"If you know how to defeat the Haunted Eye, why haven't you done it?" Antonio snapped.

"Because we are not like you martial artists," Lyric said simply. "And we do not possess the focus and spirit power of your Black Belt Club. If we did, Allaria would not have called *you*."

"That makes sense," said Jamie. "But what are we supposed to do?"

THERE IS ONLY ONE WAY TO *BREAK* THE SPELL.

THE *THIRD* GIFT?

"Yes. Listen carefully. When you see Kaelin at the Stone Circle, you must concentrate and repeat these words to him three times. The words are—"

Blam! Horns blasted outside the mound.

"The warning signal!" cried Lyric, jumping up.

We ran to the door. The Green Man was riding into the village with his herd of stags. Their antlers knocked down everything in their path. Ladders crashed to the ground, food baskets flew through the air, and the people ran for their lives. Beside the Green Man, Kaelin rode on a stag and waved his sword wildly through the air.

Lyric led us to a trapdoor.

Great! Another dark tunnel with creepy things hiding in the shadows.

The roof above us shook as a stag trampled across the mound. I jumped into the hole.

"Max? You're actually going first?" Maia asked, climbing down. Antonio and Jamie followed.

Lyric called down after us. "The tunnel is a short-cut to the Stone Circle. Now go!"

Lyric's voice echoed in the chamber. "The mind is mightier than the sword!" he yelled.

The trapdoor slammed shut behind us. Now the tunnel was pitch-black.

CHAPTER 7

THE MIND is mightier than the sword! What does that mean? I thought. I repeated it over and over so I wouldn't forget. The tunnel was cold and dark, and I couldn't see a thing. I felt a ball of fear in my stomach.

"I've changed my mind," I said. "I need to get out of here."

"Don't chicken out now, Max," said Maia.

"Yeah, man, we've got a mission," said Antonio. "We're out of time! Come on!"

I heard Antonio move ahead, but I stood frozen in place. My breath grew heavy, and it echoed in my head.

"What's wrong, Max?" I felt Jamie touch my arm. "Hey! You guys! Max is shaking."

"What's the matter, Max? Afraid of the dark?" Maia taunted.

STOP IT, MAIA.

SOMETHING'S WRONG WITH HIM.

My head was spinning. *I can't breathe!* I gasped for air.

Antonio ran back to me. "What's up, man?"

I couldn't speak. I swayed on my feet. Antonio and Jamie grabbed me and helped me sit down.

"Typical," said Maia, under her breath. "You're slowing us up, as usual."

WHAT IS IT, MAX?

Maia got quiet.

"Everything is OK, Max," said Jamie. "I used to be afraid to go into elevators because there were no windows, but I'm not afraid anymore."

I was breathing too fast. "Why not?"

"Because I meditated, the way we learned in karate," she answered. "I put myself in another place in my mind. You want to try it with me?"

"OK," I answered, still feeling dizzy.

The sound of stomping thundered overhead.

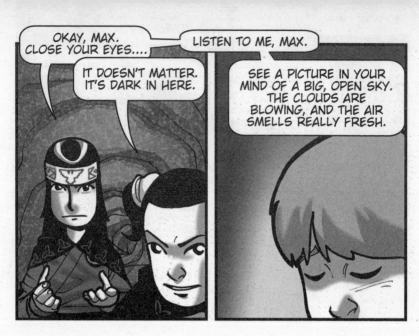

I could kind of see the sky, but I didn't smell any fresh air.

"Breathe like me and Antonio—nice and slow," she said.

I could hear them taking long, deep breaths. I listened and tried to follow. I saw the blue sky in my mind, and I was beginning to feel calmer. My breathing slowed down. The slower I breathed, the easier it was to imagine clouds blowing across the blue sky. It was working. My head stopped spinning. Jamie squeezed my hand, and Antonio patted my shoulder.

I stood up and still felt a little shaky. I had heard of claustrophobia, but this was my first experience. My dad told me that sometimes people develop fears, and it can happen anytime. *But why now?* Maia was right. I *was* slowing everyone down.

Blue sky, fresh air, floating clouds, breathe slow, I kept saying to myself. It worked. I moved forward with my friends.

"The tunnel must be taking us the right way," said Antonio. "My crystal is brighter again."

"Look, there's light up ahead," I said. *Maybe we were closer to the Stone Circle than we thought.*

The tunnel curved upward.

"It's a door to another mound. The light must be coming from a fire," said Maia.

Antonio didn't listen, and he opened the door, anyway. Suddenly, the ceiling of the tunnel ripped off, and the Green Man stood tall above us. He whipped his head around.

Maia, Jamie, and Antonio tried to duck, but they weren't quick enough. As the Green Man turned, a huge glob of eyeball juice splattered all over them. Antonio's crystal dimmed to darkness.

"Yuck!" said Maia, trying to wipe the disgusting goop off her face.

The Green Man whooped with glee. He leaned forward and tried to grab them. He was screaming in victory—or was it the Haunted Eye screaming?

"Run!" yelled Maia.

They jumped back into the hole, and we took off down the tunnel. The Green Man's arm stretched into the darkness after us. We turned a corner just in time and barely escaped his groping hand.

The walls of this tunnel were covered with gnarled roots growing down from the trees above. The ground was wet and slippery, so it was hard not to fall. We ran as fast as we could in the dark, holding on to the roots for balance.

WE MUST HAVE *MISSED* THE TUNNEL THAT GOES TO THE STONE CIRCLE WHEN ANTONIO WAS LEADING.

WHAT?

This is sounding bad. I wish I could see. I took out my crystal. Suddenly, it lit up just in time to see Maia, Antonio, and Jamie shoving one another.

"Ooh! Tough guy!" said Maia.

"I'm tougher!" said Jamie. She pushed Maia against the wall.

"Hey, guys, this tunnel must be a Ley Line. Look, my crystal lit up again."

He suddenly rammed me hard against the wall.

"Stop it, Antonio!" I said, grabbing his cape.

Then Maia and Jamie pounced. They tackled both of us to the ground.

"Get off me!" I yelled. "What are you guys doing? We're on the right track—let's go!"

We wrestled in the narrow space of the tunnel. My crystal fell to the ground. Luckily it still glowed, so I could see in the dark. Maia sat on top of me with her hands around my neck. I lifted my hip to try and throw her off, but the tunnel was too small.

Jamie and Antonio pushed each other back and forth while they yelled mean names.

This is crazy. What's happening to us? Water began dripping faster and faster from the roots around us. "Look," I said. "It must be raining up there!"

"So what?" Maia sneered. "Now you're scared of a little water? You are such a chicken."

The tunnel began to look like a shower. I saw that Maia's cape was still covered with slime from the Haunted Eye. *That must be it! The evil eye juice has made everyone lose focus and attack!*

As the water splashed out of the roots like rain, I saw the slime being washed off Maia's cape. She leaned over me, and part of it oozed onto my face. For a split second, I couldn't remember anything. I suddenly wanted to hurt Maia! I reached up and grabbed her neck when . . .

A fat root above me opened up like a faucet. Water poured all over us. I coughed and gasped for air. We were completely soaked, and everyone stopped fighting. As soon as we stopped fighting, the water stopped, too.

"What happened?" asked Antonio, shaking water from his hair.

A silvery image of Allaria appeared in the roots.

THE HAUNTED EYE HAS HAD TIME TO HYPNOTIZE MORE CREATURES OF THE FOREST. YOU MUST STOP IT BEFORE SUNRISE. HURRY!

DID YOU JUST HELP US?

"The trees are part of my spirit," she answered. "Yes. Now, go! And remember: *The mind is mightier than the sword.*" Her image faded.

I took off my cape to wring out the water. "Those are the words Lyric told us," I said.

"You're right, Max," said Jamie. "That must be the key to our mission."

Antonio punched me lightly on the shoulder.

SORRY, MAN. YOU'RE STILL MY BRO, RIGHT?

Maia reached out to help me up. *This is a good sign,* I thought.

"Thanks, Maia."

"OK, but don't get used to it."

Chomp! Chomp! Chomp!

"Max, is your stomach growling?" asked Maia.

"Not right now," I answered.

We held up our crystals, trying to see farther down the tunnel.

"Ah!" we screamed.

Glowing red eyes leered at us from the darkness.

A set of sharp teeth almost bit off my ear! Instinctively, I pivoted on my back foot. The creature ran past me.

"Whoa! A mutant animal!" said Antonio.

"It must be under the spell of the Haunted Eye!" cried Jamie.

The vicious creature slid to a quick stop, using its long claws. Red eyes glared at us. It crouched and was ready to pounce when Allaria's face appeared in the roots behind it.

As the mutant animal tried to jump, the roots closed in around it. The creature tried to chew its way out, but the roots only squeezed tighter. It hissed at us but could not escape.

"Let's move!" said Maia. "The Green Man must have sent this animal to stop us from getting to the Stone Circle before him."

"We need to focus and work as a team," said Jamie.

"I'm ready," said Antonio.

"Me, too," I said.

"Let's do it," said Maia.

We gave one another high fives. We decided to stay in ready stance and double-step down the tunnel with our guard up, just in case.

"I see light," said Antonio. "The opening must be right up there."

"How can there be light when it's dark outside?" I asked.

CHAPTER 8

THE TRAPDOOR was already open when we reached the end of the tunnel. The light outside was still a bluish color—the color of the sky when it's between night and day, before the sun rises.

"Shh!" said Maia. "Do you hear anything?"

We sat for a few minutes to make sure no one was there. Antonio climbed the ladder first and peeked out.

"All clear," he called down.

As I stepped out into the fresh air, I took a deep breath. We had entered a thick grove of trees. Since winter was now ending, many of the trees did not have leaves. Though the light was dim, I could see something through the branches.

Gigantic stones stood at attention in a perfect circle. The bright, full moon was setting in the west, while the sun was about to rise in the east. Hundreds of animals moved around the stones, waiting for the new season to begin.

LET'S GET CLOSER.
WE HAVE TO HELP THE GREEN MAN *BEFORE* THE SUN RISES.

Quietly, we slipped through the woods toward the circle of stones. The nearer we got, the more animals we saw. Rabbits, foxes, wild boars, sheep, and elk were all gathered. Horses pranced back and forth as geese rode on their backs. We saw more birds than we knew existed.

We crouched down and hid at the edge of the ring of stones. The Green Man stood in the center with his arms lifted, facing the rising sun.

KAELIN!

I tried to scramble to my feet, but Kaelin's sword was at my throat quicker than I could move.

"Everybody stand up. Put your hands on your heads, and march in a line to the center of the Stone Circle."

His sword! What was I supposed to say about his sword? Think, Max, think!

Kaelin pressed the tip a little harder against my skin. "I said, *'move it! Now!'*"

"OK. OK," I said with a choke.

We stood up and did as we were told. Antonio and Jamie went first, and Maia and I followed.

Kaelin lifted his sword and jabbed me in the back.

We were walking toward the Green Man when I heard Maia whisper to Jamie, "Time for Animal Powers."

I saw Jamie nod. Then she whispered to Antonio. He nodded, too.

How are we supposed to do that? I'm the only one holding my crystal. Their crystals are lit, but we still need a ray of light to activate our Animal Powers. The sun's not up yet! This is impossible!

I clutched the crystal in my hand. Our crystals were lit up because we were walking on a Ley Line. *That's it! Maybe if we focus really hard and say the words again, we can use the energy of the Ley Line to activate our Animal Powers!*

I heard Maia whisper, "Drop down, and get ready to use your Animal Power."

She gets it. She has the same idea!

The animals around the Stone Circle howled and squawked as if they were cheering us on. Without Kaelin's knowledge, all of us now held our glowing crystals. A spark of light flickered between them, and the image of my Bear lit up. The combined lights and the power of the Ley Lines had triggered our Animal Powers. I closed my eyes for a moment and felt my Bear strong within me. It was as if he had been waiting for me to call him. Now I was ready for anything.

I looked at the others, and they were all strong with their Animal Powers, too. Jamie lifted her arms, ready to rise into action with her Eagle. Maia stood on one leg with the perfect balance of her Crane. Antonio tipped his head down as if he had the horns of his Bull.

"Kiai!" screamed Antonio as he charged at Kaelin. Jamie followed with a flying, spinning back kick, as Maia did a jumping front kick. Before Kaelin even realized what had happened, he was on the ground. I pivoted to the right with a wheel kick and knocked the sword out of his hand. It flew through the air and stabbed the ground right next to Antonio.

THANKS, GUYS!

Antonio grabbed the sword. He lunged at Kaelin.

WAIT! WE CAN'T *HURT* HIM. WE'RE SUPPOSED TO *HELP* HIM!

Antonio stopped in his tracks, but his eyes were glowing like a bull aiming at a red cape.

Antonio took another step forward.

"Get those children!" shrieked the Haunted Eye from its perch atop the Green Man.

We turned to the center of the circle and saw six warriors. They were the same ones who had attacked us in the House of the Green Warriors.

My brain felt clouded. The sky was beginning to lighten. Soon the sun would rise. *What was it Lyric told us to say? Why won't my mind work? My mind . . . my mind. . . . Wait—that's it!*

Kaelin jumped up and tried to grab me. I did a perfect shoulder roll with the control and strength of my Bear. I jumped to my feet and shouted to Kaelin, "The mind is mightier than the sword!"

Kaelin stopped in his tracks as if he were thinking hard about what I had said.

Kaelin held his head in his hands and ripped off his helmet. He squeezed his eyes shut.

"Max! Duck!" yelled Antonio.

A camouflaged warrior flew at me with a side kick aimed at my head. I fell down hard but didn't hurt my back because I slapped my hands on the ground the moment I hit.

Jamie moved with the precision of her Eagle and dodged two warriors with a sidestep, then tripped them with a leg sweep. Maia and I turned together and knocked two more warriors to the ground with spinning back fists. Kaelin stepped toward Antonio, who was still holding the sword.

BUT YOU WERE RIGHT, ANTONIO. THE MIND *IS* MIGHTIER THAN THE SWORD.

I REMEMBER MY POWER NOW. THERE'S NO TIME TO LOSE. WE NEED TO CAPTURE THE HAUNTED EYE. LOOK! THE SUN IS *RISING!*

KAELIN IS WITH US!

QUICK!

WE MUST CIRCLE THE GREEN MAN AND TRY TO CAPTURE THE EYE BEFORE THE SUN RISES. BE CAREFUL NOT TO LOOK AT IT!

WE STILL HAVE OUR *ANIMAL POWERS!* LET'S GO!

"And we have the second gift—our capes!" yelled Jamie.

The Green Man had risen to new heights in the center of the Stone Circle. With the strength of our Animal Powers, we ran full speed at the Haunted Eye.

THE ONLY CHANCE WE HAVE IS TO TAKE OUT THE GREEN MAN'S *LEGS!*

WE'RE GOING TO HAVE TO USE SOME *SWIFT KICKS.*

A *SPINNING REVERSE WHEEL KICK* SHOULD DO IT.

Antonio reached the Green Man first and held up Kaelin's sword. "You can't escape us now!" yelled Antonio.

The Green Man tried to reach out and grab it, but every time he did, Antonio sliced the air so the Green Man couldn't get hold of it. The Haunted Eye oozed blood and screamed. "Get them!" it thundered. We didn't dare look directly at it.

I pulled up the hood of my cape so the triple-knot design would protect me from the hypnotic glare.

The Green Man's arms stretched over us as he tried to grab Kaelin. With one swift move, Kaelin snatched the sword from Antonio's hand and struck at the stringy arm just before it grabbed him. The sword sliced through a thick tangle of vines, and they fell to the ground. The arm shrank back, and the Green Man took a few steps away from us.

"Circle him!" shouted Maia.

She and Jamie swiftly moved with the power of their birds to his back side.

Working as a team, with the Animal Powers making us stronger, we struck a winning combination. The girls leaped in the air and spun around two times. Their legs smacked into the backs of the Green Man's knees like flying baseball bats. It worked!

"Argh!" he yelled, and he dropped to the ground. The Haunted Eye continued to scream, louder and louder. My ears were ringing.

The Green Man turned toward Antonio and me, and we were ready with our next moves.

LET'S KNOCK THAT SLIMEBALL OFF HIS HEAD.

The Bear and Bull were perfect together. We threw ourselves to the ground, and with a superspeed shoulder roll, we plowed into the Green Man's chest. As we flipped over, our legs smashed into the crown holding the Haunted Eye in place. It tipped sideways, nearly falling off his head.

Maia and Jamie quickly sprang into action. They vaulted to the middle of the Green Man's back and hung on to his stringy vines. He tried to push them away, but they easily dodged his sweeping hands.

The Green Man suddenly grabbed me and squeezed. I tightened my body. *I am the Bear.* I flexed my muscles. He squeezed harder, but it didn't hurt. Then he pulled me up to his face and tried to force me to look at the bulging, bleeding Haunted Eye. I thought my eardrums would burst from the scream. Quickly, the girls climbed up the Green Man's neck and grabbed hold of the back of his crown.

Maia pulled on the right side of the crown, and Jamie did a palm heel strike, hitting the left side. *Wham!* The crown slid sideways.

The Haunted Eye couldn't see us! The Green Man lowered his hand to the ground. He tried to toss me into Antonio so he could fix his crown, but Antonio and I were too quick. As soon as the Green Man let me go, we grabbed a vine from each arm and ran in superspeed circles, round and round, until we had twisted his arms into a knot.

The Green Man twisted himself in knots, trying to escape. He writhed so much that the crown finally slipped off his head. *Splat!* The Haunted Eye fell to the ground.

Goop and bloodred juice oozed into the grass.

"Yuck!" I said. "That's nasty!"

The animals surrounding the circle of stones burst into a chorus of music and joyful howling as the sun rose above the trees. The first rays of light hit the circle.

"Quick!" shouted Kaelin. "Cover the Haunted Eye! Don't let the light shine on it!"

"Cover it with what?" I asked.

We were standing in the middle of the circle of giant stones. The six camouflaged warriors had been knocked out, but they were waking up as the sunlight hit them.

"Uh-oh, guys," I said, pointing to the warriors.

"Don't worry about them," said Kaelin. "They're free from the spell now."

The Haunted Eye began to wiggle on the ground.

"It's trying to flip itself over to see the light," said Maia.

"Our capes!" I said. "Let's cover it with our capes!"

We untied them from our shoulders and threw them over the Eye—just in time. The first rays of morning light burst into the middle of the Stone Circle and flooded over all of us. It felt warm and peaceful. The Green Man began to wake up from his trance. He sat up and opened his eyes to the new day.

The creatures of the forest rejoiced with squawking, buzzing, humming, chirping, screeching, and howling. Kaelin laughed loudly as the sounds of cheer surrounded us. From the eastern archway of the circle of stones, Allaria stepped forward, holding a large cloth sack printed with the triple-knot pattern. She knelt beside the Green Man and looked into his eyes.

"I will take care of that. You have done enough, thank you," said Allaria, smiling at each of us.

She knelt down next to our capes and carefully put her gloved hand beneath them and felt for the crown. Slowly, she slipped the crown into her sack. At the same time, Kaelin untied the Green Man's arms. Soon he was covered with leaves.

The animals howled as the Green Man stood tall and smiled. He stretched his body high into the sky. He lifted his arms and laughed with happiness.

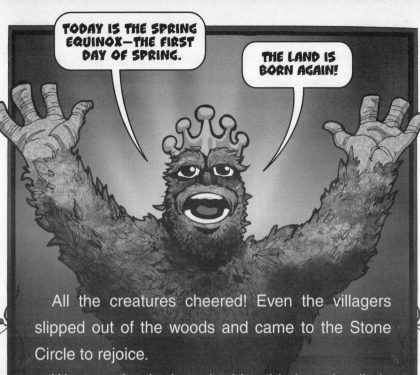

TODAY IS THE SPRING EQUINOX—THE FIRST DAY OF SPRING.

THE LAND IS BORN AGAIN!

All the creatures cheered! Even the villagers slipped out of the woods and came to the Stone Circle to rejoice.

We waved to Lyric as he blew his horn loudly in celebration.

"Thank you for helping," Allaria said to us. "We shall always be grateful. I'm sure Lyric will sing a tall tale about you."

"Sweet," said Antonio. "Our own Lyric-bard-yard rap."

Maia rolled her eyes.

Kaelin bowed to us, in the traditional, martial-arts way. "Thank you for helping our land when I so deeply failed."

"Failure is but an opportunity for growth," said Allaria, softly touching his shoulder.

Kaelin smiled gratefully and bowed to her. "Thank you, Priestess."

"Yes, thank you, Priestess Allaria," we all said and bowed.

SAFE JOURNEY HOME, YOUNG CHAMPIONS.

She turned and walked away from the Stone Circle, carrying the Haunted Eye with her.

Spring had begun all around us. New blossoms sprouted from the trees. The grass under our feet grew as we stood upon it. Baby birds squeaked hungrily for food, while the animals jumped and played with one another.

We stepped into our four directions within the ring of stones. The Circle was a powerful place. I could feel the extra energy under my feet as we began the Four Winds Kata.

The people from the village watched us. We picked up speed with each step we took. The morning sun was warm on my face. I, too, felt as if I had just come out of a cold, dark winter and had been given a fresh start. It was a new day.

And, in a flash of wind and light, we were gone.

CHAPTER 9

THE DOJO lobby was empty. It was almost dark outside. Sensei stood alone as we landed gracefully on the mats.

"Thank you," she said. "I know you were successful because my own focus has become strong again."

"Me, too," said Jamie.

"Yeah, I can even remember I have homework due tomorrow," said Antonio.

"Why was it morning there, and it's evening here?" I asked.

"Day and night, light and dark, are different in each dimension, Max."

"Huh?" I said.

"It doesn't matter," Sensei told me. "What does matter is this: Even a dark night can be a new beginning, if you want it to be."

"You sound like Priestess Allaria," said Maia.

I wanted to ask Sensei more questions, but I could see Uncle Al waiting in the car outside. I knew I'd better go.

LINE UP.

CONGRATULATIONS, *CHAMPIONS OF THE FOUR WINDS*. YOU HAVE MADE ANOTHER WORLD SAFE. YOU ARE TRULY HEROES, AND I AM *PROUD* OF YOU.

THANK YOU, SENSEI.

We bowed to one another, and we handed her our Animal Power crystals. She returned them to the Box of the Four Doors, and we said good-bye.

"Max, come here," said Maia.

She pulled me over to the corner of the room. *I hope she's not going to say something nasty to me again. I just want to go home now.*

"Um, well, I thought we made a good team. I was glad to have you with me today when we were fighting Kaelin."

Am I dreaming? What do I say? Too bad there aren't any witnesses, because nobody's going to believe this. I paused for a moment to gather my thoughts. Then I said, "Thanks, Maia. I thought so, too. See you next class."

I looked up at the window and noticed something up at the top I had never seen before. It was a crystal eye. When I focused on it, the crystal eye lit up. *Wow! The dojo is a Ley Line!* Of course! I smiled and stepped outside. As I walked over to Uncle Al's car, I saw the sky was the same color as it had been on the Isle of Oculus—or as Antonio said, "Octopus." It was that bluish color just before the sun rises—and right after the sun sets.

In Los Angeles, the sun had just set. Even though it wasn't a new day, my focus had changed. I was going to write down all the things I wanted to do—everything I wanted to focus on and make happen in my life. That way, if I ever lost my focus again, I'd have my list so I would never forget.

Things change all the time—the seasons, what people think of you, and even the way we think about ourselves. For me, what has really changed the most is this: I am more excited than ever to be part of the Black Belt Club!

BASIC KARATE TECHNIQUES

When Max Greene was training for his black belt, he practiced these karate moves. Be sure an adult is present to help you. And remember: The karate you learn here is only used for self-defense, and only when there is no other option.

FRONT KICK

SLIDE-UP SIDE KICK

PIVOTING
SIDE
KICK

STEPPING
SIDE
KICK

SPINNING BACK KICK

HOPPING BACK KICK

HOOK KICK

CRESCENT KICK

STOMP KICK

DROPPING MULE KICK

ABOUT THIS BOOK

KARATE IS a type of martial art where a student learns physical and mental discipline for balance of mind, body, and spirit. It is believed that martial arts were created several thousand years ago in China by Shaolin monks who needed a way to protect themselves from traveling warlords. Over time, martial arts evolved into hundreds of different styles that spread throughout the Far East. Some of the moves practiced in this book are based upon Shotokan karate techniques from Japan. The word karate means "empty hand," because we learn how to protect ourselves without using weapons. Karate is a great way to get in shape, to gain confidence, and to have fun! To learn more, check your library, the Internet, or www.theblackbeltclub.com.

The story line for *Beware of the Haunted Eye* uses several elements of ancient Celtic civilization. More than two thousand years ago, most of Europe north of the Mediterranean was dominated by Celts. The Celts kept records of their history through oral storytelling, song, dance, and art. Since very little was written down, not much is known about their ancient culture, but they left behind beautiful gold jewelry and decorated weaponry. Art historians have collected pottery and artifacts embellished with the triple-knot design, which was believed to ward off the "evil eye." The "Green Man" still decorates buildings and monuments throughout Europe. Ley Lines are energy patterns under the ground, and people often built ceremonial temples on them. The labyrinth is reflective of the triple-knot pattern used to confuse evil energy. Lyric, in this story, is a bard who would have recorded clan history through song.

The Celts were fearsome warriors, but a High Priestess was often followed for religious ceremonies, especially those that honored the changing of the seasons. Throughout Great Britain there are still giant stone circles where it is thought Solstice and Equinox celebrations took place.

DAWN BARNES is a third-degree black belt in Shotokan karate, and she is the founder of Dawn Barnes Karate Kids, the most successful all-children's karate school in the United States. She produces instructional DVDs and manuals, and she lectures nationally in the martial arts. Sensei Dawn was recently inducted in the Black Belt Hall of Fame as Woman of the Year 2006. She lives in Los Angeles with her family and two dogs. This is her third book. Email her at www.theblackbeltclub.com. BERNARD CHANG began his career in the comic book world, where his work on such popular characters as Doctor Mirage, Superman, and the X-Men earned him a coveted spot on the top ten artists in *Wizard: The Guide to Comics*. He lives in Los Angeles.

SOME KARATE TERMS

WORD	PRONUNCIATION	MEANING
dojo	doe-joh	karate school
gi	gee	karate uniform
ki	kee	spirit
kiai	kee-eye	spirit power
sensei	sen-say	karate teacher
osu	oss	yes, I understand
kiotsuki, rei	kee-o-skay, ray	attention, bow

FOR MORE KARATE MOVES...

read the first two books in The Black Belt Club series: *Seven Wheels of Power* and *Night on the Mountain of Fear*. In those books, you will see the following: upward block, x-block, inward block, downward block, front kick, side kick, back kick, straight punch, palmheel strike, hammerfist strike, roundhouse kick, wheel kick, jab/reverse strike, back knuckle strike, hook kick, forward shoulder roll, pivoting side kick, mule kick, jumping side kick, and hopping front kick.

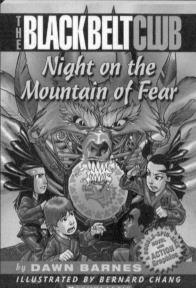